THE
TABLECLOTH
TRICK

THE
TABLECLOTH
TRICK

A FICTION

RICK CRILLY

MISFIT

ECW Press

Published by ECW PRESS
2120 Queen Street East, Suite 200, Toronto, Ontario, Canada M4E 1E2

LIBRARY AND ARCHIVES CANADA CATALOGUING IN PUBLICATION

Crilly, Rick
The tablecloth trick / Rick Crilly.

"A misFit book".

ISBN 978-1-55022-770-3

1. Title.

PS8605.R54T32 2007   C813'.6   C2006-906798-8

Editor for the press: Michael Holmes
Cover and Text Design: Tania Craan
Cover Image: Haig Bedrossian
Illustrations: Haig Bedrossian and Kyra Crilly
Typesetting: Mary Bowness
Printing: Coach House Printing

This book is set in Adobe Garamond

The publication of *The Tablecloth Trick* has been generously supported by the Canada
Council, the Ontario Arts Council, and the Government
of Canada through the Book Publishing Industry
Development Program.

DISTRIBUTION
CANADA: Jaguar Book Group, 100 Armstrong Ave., Georgetown, ON L7G 5S4

PRINTED AND BOUND IN CANADA

ECW PRESS
ecwpress.com

for Kyra

1. The Man with an
Unclean Spirit
(1:23-26)
2. Healing Simon's
Mother-in-Law
(1:30-31)
3. Healing a Leper
(1:40-45)
4. Healing Palsey
(2:1-12)
5. The Withered Hand
(3:1-6)
6. Stilling the Storm
(4:35-41)
7. The Gadarene
Demoniac
(5:1-20)
8. The Daughter of Jarius
(5:21-43)
9. The Afflicted Woman
(5:25-34)
10. Feeding the Five
Thousand
(6:30-46)
11. Jesus Walking on
the Water
(6:47-56)
12. Syrophoenician
Woman's Daughter
(7:24-30)

Page 20: "In 1885, Robert Wiedersheim listed 180 alleged vestigial or rudimentary organs in man, today the list is down to a handful: tonsils, adenoids, coccyx, nictating membrane of eye, thymus, appendix, little toe, wisdom teeth, nipples on males, parathyroid, nodes on ears (Darwin's points), auricular muscles, body hair, pineal gland." — *Snakes with Hipbones and Whale Hind Legs*, Jon A. Covey

13. Deaf and Dumb Man
(7:31-37)
14. Feeding the Four
Thousand
(8:1-9)
15. The Blind Man Near
Bethsaida
(8:22-26)
16. The Demoniac Boy
(9:14-29)
17. The Blind Men
Near Jericho
(10:46-52)
18. The Withered
Fig Tree
(11:20-25)

Programmed Cell Death *or* Religion is a Compulsory Credit Course

August 1977: in the Reference Only section of the Winnipeg Centennial Library.

Caroline was amassing evidence to debunk the eighteen supposed miracles of Jesus recorded in the Gospel according to Mark.

I was reading a book on vestigial organs.

I placed the book on the table.

It looked like a tent supported on poles.

I couldn't stop smiling.

"What is it?" Caroline asked.

"It's . . . well . . . watch," I said.

And using the three muscles of the scalp that Darwin called "useless,"[1] I wiggled my ears.

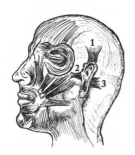

I was born premature (4 pounds, 5 ounces) with a two-inch tail appended to my spine, which doctors postponed removing because of my diminutive size and as a result were unable to detach it, fearing by then the cartilaginous elements had become too essential a component of my vertebral column.

I was also born colour-blind and Roman Catholic.

At six years old, I had determined for myself the inability to see red. I was watching *The Wizard of Oz* with my brother, an annual event. We were sitting cross-legged on the living room floor in front of the television. The ghost of Charley Becker[2] was wedged between us. An important question had just presented itself: "the colour of Dorothy Gale's ruby slippers[1]?"

"Give them back to me!" the Wicked Witch of the West exclaimed.

"It's too late!" declared Good Glinda from the North, "There they are and there they'll stay," referring to the high-heeled shoes on Dorothy's feet. "Keep tight inside of them . . . their magic must be very powerful, or she wouldn't want them so badly."

---

[2] According to the Fort Garry Lance, the house I grew up in was originally the home of actor Charley Becker, who as Mayor of Munchkin City had verified "legally, morally, ethically, spiritually, physically, absolutely, positively, undeniably, and reliably," the Wicked Witch of the East, "dead."

Up until the age of three, Caroline's right hand was webbed: "complete simple syndactylism." Surgery was performed to separate the fingers. At fourteen, she still had the zigzag scars to prove it.[3]

3

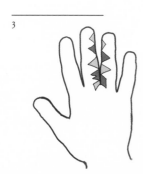

The last evening before the start of high school, in the garden behind
Caroline's house on Jupiter Bay[4] — amidst white trumpet-shaped
blooms that emitted perfume only at night, and a shared belief system
that all life originated in the sea — we had wrapped ourselves in a
blanket.

There was a big oak in Caroline's backyard called the Cancer Tree,
because no matter what her father did to it, it kept growing into
infinity.

On the tree's trunk was a simulacrum of the Virgin Mary — and,
depending on your vantage point (based on the time of day and dif-
fering angles and shadows), the Virgin Mary was either holding the
infant Jesus or the puppet Pinocchio.

The dayside of the Tree: "When the chief priests and the officers
saw him, they cried out, 'Crucify him! Crucify him!'"[5]

The nightside of the Tree: "'I see what we must do!' said one of the
assassins. 'He must be hung! Let us hang him!'" [6 II]

---

4 "In the 1950s, an inspired developer observed a similarity between the curving streets
in his new neighbourhood and the orbit of heavenly bodies. So, he created a suburban
galaxy, Jupiter and Saturn Bays, Mars Drive, and even Pluto Street." — Michele
Peterson
5 John, 19:34
6 *The Adventures of Pinocchio,* Chapter xv, Carlo Collodi

Caroline's mother wore a blue wig to conceal hair loss during chemotherapy.[7]

7

Two weeks into Grade 9, Caroline found a note in her locker.[8] It was a copy of the note astronaut John Glenn had carried in 1962 in the event his capsule crashed into the South Pacific on reentry.[III]

Caroline said the note was from a boy with the same name as her mother. I knew her mother only as Mrs. Bayes. She died when we were young.

I found out who the boy was in English class. I saw Caroline pass him a note of her own.

He had pigtails because Principal Sister Elisabeth was trying to shame him into cutting his hair.

All the girls thought he was cute. The boys were scared shitless of him.

He was Caroline's first love.

---

[8] *I am a stranger. I come in peace. Take me to your leader and there will be a massive reward for you in eternity.*

I loved her but to her we were just friends.

Around the time of Mrs. Bayes's death (I was nine), my father replaced all the mirrors in our house with trick mirrors from a fun-house. The mirror in my little brother's room reproduced muscles of superhero size. Unfortunately, my little brother ended up measuring wider than he did high. The mirror in my room had the opposite effect. I grew taller, from three feet to six feet, and skinny like pulled taffy. Eventually I lost all appetite. My mother was the least lucky. When she stepped in front of her dresser she sprouted a huge chin, butt and thighs. She became obese.

Unbeknownst to my father, who by and large remained unaltered (his hair had always possessed the reflecting quality of silver),[9] the mirrors were used against him as covert devices via the alchemy of urine.[10][IV] Later, when my mother discovered our secret, having once and for all sniffed out the source of that acrid smell, she was emphatic we must use lemon juice, "which contains similar properties," she said. And the mirrors, although easier to clean, never stopped preaching at us because of it.

---

9 "Hair silvering is called canities. There is no such thing as grey hair for as soon as a hair is incapable of producing coloured pigment it grows white." — hair-science.com

10 Uric acid, when introduced to heat (using a match or lighter), provided my brother and me with a hidden way to communicate.

Growing up, I was never allowed to have friends over. Mom said it was because my father liked his privacy.

Caroline was my first friend. We met in Grade 1. She lived right around the corner so I spent most of my time at her house.

After Caroline's mother died, Mr. Bayes started taking us to the library on Saturdays, where he would disappear for hours.

I think Caroline read every book ever written on cancer.

The British Museum Book of Ancient Egypt. Spells and Spellcraft. Mathematics Made Easy. Chronicle of the Maya Kings and Queens. Charlottetown Canada's Birthplace. Whistle like a Bird. The Big Strawberry Book of Space. Diving for Sunken Treasure. Fun with Chemistry. The Illustrated Encyclopedia of the World's Great Movie Stars. Healing Herbs and Plants. Blackstone's Modern Card Tricks. Flying Aces of World War I. Atlas of Human Anatomy. The Nag Hammadi Library. Time Warps. Weather Forecasting. Puzzling Questions about Death. How to Make a Paper Airplane. Hardy Boys #3: The Secret of the Old Mill. Numerology. What Modern Hypnotism Can Do For You. The Bermuda Triangle. Making Noah's Ark Toys in Wood. 19th Century Medical Curios. Reincarnation. Mysteries of Atlantis. What Color is Camouflage? Labyrinths: Selected Stories & Other Writings. The Book of Jubilees. Joy of Photography. Making Sex. Bread of Dreams. The Great Houdini. John Dee's Conversations with Angels. Paganism. Beekeeping. Paradise Lost. Torah. Qur'an. Holy Bible. Ovid's Metamorphoses. Color Theory. History of Art. Gulliver's Travels. Unicorns. Phantom Islands of the Pacific Ocean. The Penguin Atlas of Endangered Species. Louis Riel. Sir Francis Bacon. Nostradomus. Expert Judo. Montezuma's Mexico. Trees in Canada. April Raintree. Locomotion. Dracula. The Medici. Tracking Marco Polo. Exploring the Moon through Binoculars. Ice Fishing. Lives of the Saints. Classical Mythology. Forbidden Archeology. The Way Things Work. The Three Musketeers. The Divine Comedy. Vikings. Geronimo. Mystical Qabalah. Arabian Nights. Carnivorous Plants of the World. Galileo. Milk Pitcher Magic. Freud. Grimm's Fairy Tales. ESP. The Theory of Relativity. Stalin. The Indians of Canada. Wildflowers. Rameau's Nephew. Catechism of the Catholic Church. Plato: Republic. Snakes with

Hipbones and Whale Hind Legs. Hans Christian Anderson. The Art of War. Jack the Ripper. Inventory of Greek Coin Hoards. How to be a Happy Conductor of Choirs. Palmistry. The Anatomy of Melancholy. Cezanne. How We Think. Rider Waite Tarot. Herodotus. Alice in Wonderland. Stamps of the World. Trollology. Cartooning. The Oxford English Dictionary. Dolphins. Field Guide to Demons. Mysticism of Sound and Music. The Hero with a Thousand Faces. World Guide to Nude Beaches. The Prince. Homosexuality. Ancient Languages. Was/Is. Landmarks of Lower Fort Garry. Origami. Natural History. Cannibal Stars. America B.C. Volcanoes and their Activity. The Histrionic Mr. Poe. Ulysses. Cosmology. Jam Can Curling. Eros and Magic in the Renaissance. The Discovery of Guiana. Feng Shui. Herculine Barbin. Quantum Mechanics. The School of Night. Genghis Khan. Ham Radios. Metaphysics. Mummies and the Pharaohs. The Tibetan Book of the Dead. Bartholomew Parr's London Medical Dictionary. Lucretius. Hippocrates. Galen. Johannes Kepler. Mohave Desert. Halley's Comet. X-ray Radiation. Crocodiles. Arthropods. Gorillas. Mesopotamia. Influenza. Plutarch. Don Quixote. Latin Sexual Vocabulary. Leonardo da Vinci. The Dialogic Imagination. Hopi Indians. Giordano Bruno. The Annotated History of Jesting. The Practical Pendulum Book. Basic Principles of Fission Reactors. A Dictionary of Military Terms. The Philosophy of Friedrich Nietzsche. The Lone Ranger. Frankenstein. The Life Treasury of American Folklore. The Story of the Dead Sea Scrolls. History under the Sea. Joseph Cornell. TNT Mind Power. The Fictional Universe. Stonehenge. Pirahnas. Mapping Marshes. The Nickel Mines of Thompson Manitoba.

> **Library** is **Bread** or **Pyramid**
> — Jorge Luis Borges

15

There was no Tree of the Knowledge of Good and Evil. Eve plucked a metaphorical apple.[V] She carried twins in her womb. And Cain, who was the oldest, took on the characteristics of his father, Eve's *true love*, between a man and a chimpanzee.

Plato saw love as the medium through which human beings pursue transcendence. He called it the *Highest Good*.

Ovid said of love and its thousand postures to delight that what the lover truly seeks is sexual euphoria.

The Catholic Catechism equates love with service and adulation, and orders its adherents to love God above all things, and "to acknowledge in respect and absolute submission the nothingness of the creature who would not exist but for *Him*."

To scientists, the molecular basis of love is phenylethylamine and oxytocin. Phenylethylamine levels in the brain are maximally determined at puberty or in the time of *first love*.

In the *Anatomy of Melancholy*, Robert Burton described the kind of love I had for Caroline as "a Disease, Phrensy, Madness, Hell." (Unrequited.)

As a teenager, I spent much of my free time in the library reading books that fired my imagination. For me, the library was a source of unlimited discovery and wild adventure. It also kept me from dwelling on Caroline's increasing number of boyfriends.

In the library, I was a Hardy Boy, voyageur, and deep-sea diver. I calculated the distance between Hell and Heaven.[II] I learned the moon was once a land mass of the Earth whereupon a huge basin now sits called the Pacific Ocean. In theory, I was able to travel through time, hypnotize people, and ice-fish. I knew the effects of radiation exposure on A-bomb survivors.[VI] I could perform magic tricks.

Sometimes I alternated between two books, and hybrid ideas[12] presented themselves, or I focused on a particular subject[13] [VII] and buried myself in research.

I knew things that other kids didn't.

I was an active participant in my own education.

[II] In *Paradise Lost*, Lucifer's fall through Chaos lasted nine days, "Hurled headlong flaming from th' Ethereal Sky."

In *The Divine Comedy*, it was the impact of Lucifer hitting the Earth that formed Hell — a funnel-shaped hole.

Using Newtonian Laws of gravity and motion, if the moon stopped travelling in circles its fall to earth would take 4.5 days or about half the time Milton said it took Lucifer to fall, and so if Dante's Inferno is located below and the moon is 238,657 miles away, then Heaven's distance must be twice that.

12

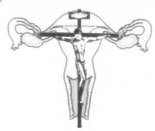

[13] e.g., The history of barbed wire.

Caroline was never my girlfriend, but on the last day of high school, in May of 1981, I asked her to be my wife.

She looked at me cautiously before responding. "Why would I?"

"Because," I fervently declared. "I've loved you since . . . forever, that's why."

Forever was twelve years.

I said: "The zodiac has twelve signs, a year twelve months. The Book of Revelation says Mary wore a crown of twelve stars. There were twelve tribes of Israel, twelve labours of Heracles, and twelve apostles for Jesus. The human body has twelve sets of ribs,[14] and the minute hand of a clock turns twelve times faster than the hour hand."[15]

---

[14] "'And he took one of his ribs; that is, the thirteenth rib on his right side.' Men have commonly as anatomists observed twelve ribs on a side. Chimpanzees and gorillas have thirteen." — John Gill

[15] Some more twelves (from Wikipedia): twelve notes in an octave, twelve people on a jury, twelve steps in Alcoholics Anonymous, the twelve days of Christmas, twelve eggs to a dozen (a sales unit in trade). And the twelve times Caroline said no to my request of marriage — just so I understood.

If knowledge is power, my most important knowledge was the knowledge that allowed me to forget. After high school, I built a memory palace[16] and locked Caroline in a closet where she lived for a year and began her studies in Philosophy before moving to British Columbia.

I got a job at Estella's Pie in the Sky Bakery. My responsibilities included anything that required proofing or fermentation, as well as a daily turnout of pie and tart shells. Kneading by hand when the recipe required it, my palms lightly dusted in flour, I learned to make a variety of leavened breads and buns, loaves absent of crust or crunchy with nuts, miraculously transformed when braided together.

If an architect decides how the world is to look, then surely a baker holds dominion over its appetite. Workers paid in bread, referred to by the Greeks as *Artophagoi* (bread eaters), built the pyramids of ancient Egypt.

According to the Gospel of St. Matthew, Jesus told a parable that went: "The kingdom of heaven is like yeast, which a woman took and hid in three measures of flour until it was all leavened." Yeast is a living organism that thrives on sugar and can be killed by too much salt or heat.

---

[16] The Renaissance technique of remembering anything by constructing an imaginary castle or palace that contains objects representing information.

While working for Estella, I got to know her history. I even considered her my friend.

She was convinced her anosmic husband was cheating on her. "Because how can he be loyal if he can't smell me?" she said.

The mornings when she wasn't expounding "anosmia patients are adulterers," she would recount some strangely wonderful story from her past. Like how in 1969 on the 20th day of July, "the most amazing day on earth," she emphasized, while the world watched the first manned lunar landing huddled around their television sets, she and Ballard Ols, were making formal their fifteen-month pledge to marry in one of those little quickie wedding chapels in Las Vegas, Nevada. But before the Apollo XI space module splashed down, rather anticlimactically into the Pacific Ocean some four days after their vows were spoken, Estella had already filed for divorce.

"Suddenly he was a different man," she told the old Mexican pawnbroker who appraised her engagement ring and wedding band.

"The night he proposed, he told me the diamond was of a rare cosmic origin. A particle of interstellar matter that had hitched a ride to Earth on something he called a chondritic meteorite."

She had to work remarkably hard to sell those rings, rendering enough money for a winning run of blackjack, prior to squandering it all at the roulette wheel.

"And where, due to good fortune or ill fate, my head spinning in orbit, under a Plexiglas solar system with a neon sun, I met my second husband, Felix Rosebrook," she said.

He was from Canada, much older than she was, and made his living going door-to-door selling MAX Factor Cosmetics. He had won a trip to Las Vegas because his sales were the highest of the Upper 49th region. An all-expense-paid week at Jack Factor's Stardust Resort and Casino. He was an unschooled, hard-working man who was willing to spend every penny he had to keep his young wife contented and who openly believed the moon landing was faked and that the earth was flat.[VIII]

"I moved in with him — into the house where his parents lived — on Water Avenue here in Winnipeg," she said. "Before the 1950 flood[IX] Felix says Water Avenue was called Assembly of God Lane. He also claims to have turned up over the years about a hundred castaway objects left behind by the Red River. Inexplicable things like a Peter Pan Potato Head, and a gold coin showing the Eastern and Western hemispheres bearing a Spanish insignia meaning 'more beyond.'"

But what really fascinated Estella was the flower garden that grew wild in the backyard. Garnish for her high-priced wedding cakes: silver-leafed psoralea, blazing big star, goldenseal, bluetongue. "I'm of a mind one night," she said, "to paint the entire garden with egg wash and sprinkle sugar all over it."

If Heaven was amidst the yeast and flour mixtures, the proofer never proved it before the oven destroyed it and all the yeast cells[17] were dead, having helped bring into being thousands of loaves of bread.[18]

[17] *Saccharomyces cerevisiae.*
[18] "Estella's Pie in the Sky Bakery lures customers with the heavenly aroma of freshly baked bread. In the morning, try muffins, sticky buns, cookies, and fresh bagels."
— *The Winnipeg Free Press*

Magic bag, Magic ball, Magic bean, Magic belt, Magic Bike, Magic book, Magic Box, Magic Breast Mound, Magic brew, Magic broom, Magic bus, Magic Cafe, Magic cap, Magic card tricks, Magic carpet, Magic carpet bag, Magic Carpet Ride, Magic castle, Magic Chalk, Magic circle, Magic City, Magic City Blues Society, Magic City Morning Star, Magic Company, Magic Converter, Magic Costumes, Magic Country, Magic cubes, Magic cup, Magic Cyber Camera, Magic Daily News, Magic Dirt, Magic dew, Magic Dragon, Magic dust, Magic Earth, Magic 8 Ball, Magic 89.9, Magic Elf, Magic Engine, Magic Eye, Magic Factory, Magic fan, Magic Fire Music, Magic Flare, Magic flower, Magic flute, Magic forest, Magic formula, Magic Foundation, Magic Fountain, Magic Garden, Magic hat, Magic Hat Brewing Company, Magic Holidays, Magic House, Magic Hypercubes, Magic Inc., Magic Index, Magic Infinity Ball, Magic Inkwell, Magic Island, Magic Johnson, Magic Key, Magic Kingdom, Magic kit, Magic Kitchen, Magic lantern, Magic Library, Magic Love Ball Keychain, Magic Mail Monitor, Magic Man, Magic Marker, Magic Math Kingdom, Magic Millions, Magic mirror, Magic Moment, Magic Mountain, Magic Movies, Magic mushroom, Magic Mystical Tour, Magic Network, Magic Newswire, Magic night, Magic number, Magic Oracle, Magic paintbrush, Magic pebble, Magic Pencil, Magic Point, Magic Pony, Magic potion, Magic power, Magic Product Inc., Magic realism, Magic ring, Magic Safaris, Magic Sand, Magic School Bus, Magic Scroll, Magic secret, Magic Service Desk, Magic Shadow Shapes, Magic shoes, Magic shop, Magic show, Magic slipper, Magic smile, Magic Soaps, Magic Software, Magic spell, Magic Spice, Magic Springs, Magic Square, Magic squirrel, Magic Stable, Magic Stars, Magic Stick, Magic stone, Magic store, Magic Surfboard, Magic sword, Magic Systems, Magic Theater, Magic Times, Magic touch, Magic Travel Group, Magic Tree House, Magic Triangles, Magic trick, Magic Tutor, Magic TV, Magic Vanishing cream, Magic Velvets, Magic Vinyl Printing, Magic Wand,

— Roland Barthes[x]

23

In the fall of 1990, I chanced upon Caroline in the lobby of the St. Boniface General Hospital. It was a catastrophe.[19]

She was scheduled to see her physician that afternoon.
"Nothing to be concerned with," she assured me.
I was visiting my sick brother.
"You know if a woman sleeps around she's more susceptible to . . ."
"God, Caroline, if I was to tally up all the women?" I lied.
But susceptible to what? I thought. Chlamydia? Cervical cancer? Infidelity?

Since moving back to Winnipeg eleven months ago, she'd been living in a low-rent apartment relying on the financial help of her father. When I asked her about Vancouver, she said, "Let's just say I'm better off."

She was working at a grocery store, fifteen hours a week, running a register. She was considering going back to school.

She talked about her dad and all the great things he had done for her — he loved her, cared for her, he forgave her — even though she continued to mess up.

After which, I had no reply. Not a word.
I noticed she kept looking at her watch.
She promised to call.
But I had to wait forever it seemed before I heard from her again.
I bought an answering machine. I wanted to be able to leave the house and not feel guilty. When I wasn't at work, I was home listening for the phone. I screened my calls so she wouldn't get a busy signal.

---

[19] "Mathematicians call a catastrophe — the disturbance of one system by another."
— Pasolini/Barthes

Her message said simply, "I will call you back," and much later, she did, to tell me she was going into the hospital for surgery tomorrow. It was 10:30 p.m. Wednesday. I was stunned.

In a Simple Mastectomy the affected breast is removed but none of the lymph nodes.[XI]

I visited her on Thursday armed with flowers.[20]

"Think of yourself as a young girl growing into a new and exciting body," said an abundantly endowed nurse. I was standing, unnoticed, between the doorframes of Caroline's hospital room, her Get Well bouquet hanging heavily at my side, my reedy bug legs especially weary, knee-deep in insecticide.

On Friday she was discharged. I gave her a ride. When we got to her apartment — she lived in the basement of a five storey building on Assinaboine Avenue — she immediately stripped down and stood in front of the mirror, "This is me," she said. We went into the shower and I used the sprayer to rinse her off. She couldn't raise her arms above the shoulder level. I washed and dried her hair. I helped dress her in loose-fitting clothes. She blamed her breast cancer on genetics. She'd been plagued with fibrocystic disease her whole life. Her first mammogram was at age twenty, "the calcifications looked like a cluster of faint stars."

---

[20] Six bright Germinis, three dark blue delphinium, three stems of chrysanthemums, yellow Solidago, purple statice, and greens.

I asked her where her father was. "I haven't told him about anything," she said. "I remember we were all sitting at the dining room table. My mother was worried. She'd never been allergic to anything in her life. Dad just went on smiling like he always did.

'Wigs nowadays, who can tell the difference,' he said. Mom ended up choosing a curly blue wig. She said it was to help maintain her sense of humour. I noticed as soon as she put it on that a certain lustre from my dad's eyes went out. A light I had taken for granted. It was the moment he gave up hope. And I was absolutely terrified."

I assured Caroline I would be there for her in whatever way she needed me. I had taken great pleasure in assisting her.

She kissed me and gave me a strong hug.

But over the course of her chemotherapy and radiation treatment she just wanted me to spend time with her doing things like watching television or going for a walk.

At the end of June 1991, before the start of her second cycle of chemotherapy,[XII] for whatever reason, she let me make love to her.

Then she went away.

To her surprise (and mine), she had openly declared a deep longing for her husband.

A famous painting by the great artist Rembrandt entitled Bathsheba at Her Bath (1654) inadvertently captured the dark shadow of cancer in the left breast. It is believed that the model used by him for this painting died from breast cancer shortly thereafter.[21]

"A thousand paper birds," I remembered Caroline saying. "The Japanese believe a crane can live up to a thousand years, and if you fold a thousand paper cranes, you will be protected from illness a thousand years." She had borrowed a copy of *The Art of Origami* from the school library. But lacking the necessary dexterity, she was finding the crane-folding instructions frustratingly involved.

"It's simple," I explained, folding one edge of the paper to meet the other, and laying it flat against the table, repeating it twice, then bringing in the corners while curling the top part under, flipping the paper over and over to form the head. "There, our first of a thousand paper cranes," I promised, pulling the fragile wings outward from the body. The day of her mother's funeral we added them up. The total: 900.

From The D. O. Hebb Lecture, V. S. Ramachandran, Center for Brain and Cognition, University of California: *"Phantom Limb* is most commonly reported following amputation of the breast, parts of the face, and sometimes even internal viscera, e.g. one can have sensations of bowel movement and flatus after a complete removal of sigmoid colon and rectum. Phantom erections can also occur in paraplegics as well as in patients who have had the penis removed." From The Prophecy Institute: "Continuing in this vein, tumours or neurological disturbances can produce the sensation of an entire phantom body."

I was able to get Caroline's Burnaby address from her father and write her a letter, but it was returned to me, unopened, marked through with a blue pen, clear as a catastrophe[22] — DOES NOT LIVE HERE.

---

[22] "Clear as a catastrophe." — Roland Barthes

*Everything has been said about the
Mona Lisa (Leonardo da Vinci took
ten years[23] to complete the lips): that
it is a self-portrait, a mistress por-
trait, a male lover, a woman who
had breast cancer or who was
bereaved or pregnant or both.[24]*

∫

*Lorenz Heister was one of the great
German surgeons in the first half of
the eighteenth century and favoured
the use of a "guillotine machine" to
rapidly remove the diseased breast. It
was purported he got the idea while
on visit to the Royal Society of
London's Arundel House in the
Museum of Curiosities from a sketch
by Leonardo da Vinci.[25]*

---

[23] "In the case of ductal carcinoma, these are called intraductal carcinoma, ductal carcinoma in situ, or noninvasive carcinoma. It is believed that breast cancer begins with
a few abnormal cells and it takes between one and ten years for these cells to reproduce
enough to make a detectable lump." — Becky Zuckweiler, MS, RN, *Living in the
Postmastectomy Body*

[24] David Allen Brown, curator of Italian Renaissance painting at the National Gallery
of Art in Washington, D.C.

[25] Dr. Paul G. Jenko, general surgeon of glioblastoma multiforme, Watson Clinic,
Lakeland, Florida

Early in July, I went to the Post Mastectomy and Bra Fitting Clinic, a support group that met at the Church of St. Agatha[26] on the first and third Wednesdays of every month from 7 to 8:30 p.m.

The meeting was in the church basement in a fusty room called Fellowship Hall. Inside the room were two folding tables lined horizontally with chairs on either side.

I counted eight women.

They were busy tossing back and forth symbolic-allegorical notions of a white circle on a chalkboard.

Because of its symmetry, the circle in nature is the perfect shape.

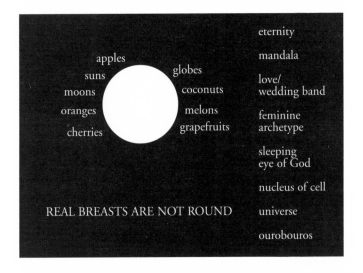

eternity

apples
mandala
suns
globes
moons
coconuts
love/
wedding band
oranges
melons
cherries
grapefruits
feminine
archetype

sleeping
eye of God

nucleus of cell

REAL BREASTS ARE NOT ROUND
universe

ourobouros

I introduced myself and felt vastly out of place but once the discussion got to breast forms and attachable nipples they hardly took notice of me.

I watched, and listened, and contributed nothing. The whole thing seemed like a hallucination.

Matildhe Milord was the group's facilitator. She was a trained nurse fitter and a stage-three survivor of two years. She had strapped a heavy-duty bra to a dress form and was demonstrating why extra fabric was needed between the cups.

Matildhe, like the rest of these women, had chosen not to have reconstruction surgery preferring a prosthetic, or padded bra, or — as Caroline had decided after visiting St. Agatha's[27] two Wednesdays in June — to do nothing.

The mastectomy side of Caroline's chest remained flat.

27

Matildhe claimed that, in 1967, she was Canada's first recipient of implanted breasts. Silicone gel packs that took her from a C cup to Double D, and from barmaid to buxom pin-up girl. When one ruptured in 1973, she was forced to have them removed, and ten years later was awarded a substantial settlement from the company that manufactured them.

"But by that time it was already too late," she said. "Never mind connective-tissue disease or autoimmune deficiencies, the result of too many men having touched them — not leaked silicone — inevitably made me sick. Man and his contagion always manage to finagle a way in, maladies such as vaginosis and pelvic inflammation, which are routinely treated with yogurt or antibiotics, to the not-so-curable diseases like AIDS and cancer. How many breast-obsessed men had I obliged, consequently putting my health at risk by simply allowing them a little grope?"

I left the meeting early and emerged into a dark, overcast night — St. Peter's Apocalypse I jokingly told myself — "flesh devouring worms so many in number as to form a colossal black cloud."

My car was in the parking lot in back of the church.

It started to rain.

Notably missing were "the unquenchable fires and gigantic lightening bolts; unchaste women with their genitals cut out hanging by their hair, their fornicators strung up by their loins."

During the drive home, I stopped at the library and borrowed a book on Greek mythology. I was thinking about the Amazon tribes. I knew that according to the legend they were a nation of female warriors, Amazon-derived from Greek meaning "without a breast," because they would voluntarily cut off one of their breasts in order to improve their fighting skills.

The rest of the way home, whenever the car was in motion, I watched raindrops on the passenger-side window turn into racing sperm and rocket ships.[28] XIII

28

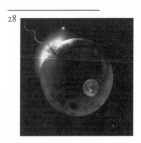

*In the left breast of Michelangelo's
figure of Night, there are three
abnormalities associated with locally
advanced cancer: an obvious, large
bulge to the breast contour medial to
the nipple; a swollen nipple-areola
complex; and an area of skin
retraction just lateral to the nipple.
These features indicate a tumor just
medial to the nipple, involving
either the nipple itself, or the
lymphatics just deep to the nipple,
and causing tethering and retraction
of the skin on the opposite side.*[29]

[29] Dr. James Stark, medical director of the Cancer Treatment Centers of America in
Portsmouth, Virginia

Heracles raped the Amazon queen Hippolyta and captured her golden girdle. It was his ninth labour. When the Amazons retaliated against him, they were all killed.

As a child, Caroline was fascinated with night-flying moths.[XIV] We were in her mother's moon garden.[30] There were silver moths whirling around us. I touched her right breast with my right hand.[XV] She told me to stop, that it was bad for me to touch her there.

---

30 "Flower choices for a moon garden: angel's trumpet *Datura innoxia;* moonflower, *Ipomoea alba;* flowering tobacco, *Nicotiana;* night-blooming silene; evening primrose, *Oenothera;* evening stock, *Matthiola bicornis;* night-blooming pea; honeysuckle; 'Silver Mound', wormwood; Japanese daylily, tuberose, *Polinathes;* Oriental lily, 'Casablanca'; white pampas grass, *Cortaderia selloana;* ornamental sage, *Salvia;* sweet woodruff; *Caladium,* 'White Queen'; dusty miller, *Cineraria;* lavender cotton, *Santolina.*" — from Llewellyn's *Moon Sign Book & Lunar Planting Guide,* 1975

Art Therapy

iv:

Raphael's La Fornarina lives in a
Roman palace now,
touching her left breast, holding it
between thumb and forefinger
like a fruit she wants to prod in the
market.
Perhaps the artist asked her to
demonstrate,
beckoning a lover,
plumping up the smaller breast,
showing off in front of the mirror.
You think she's coy.
Perhaps she wanted to touch
the lump she noticed yesterday.
Her eyes look surprised.[31]

A
GIANT
Dead
Fish[32]

---

[32] "Soon we will leave one age (Pisces) and enter into another (Aquarius). The last one coincided with the arrival of Christ. The ancients pictured Aquarius as a man pouring water from his pitcher into the open mouth of a bloated fish — Pisces."
— David Weitzman

I read somewhere that a human life can hold up to 3000 stories, no more — the same number of stars visible to the naked eye — which explains why some people live to 100 while others are pulled from the womb still-dead. Our most important stories are the ones experienced in utero — where, once upon a time, pharyngeal pouches become glands and ducts instead of gill slits, tails vanish (but for some), and aortic arches transform into arteries.

Why I ever believed in a deity, I do not know, especially one as cruel as to have cast me as a bestial adversary between man and Himself.

Father Dul: "Good Catholic children don't grow tails, son."[33]

A true human tail with blood vessels, vertebrae and cartilage is rare. Only thirty-seven cases have been reported in medical literature, worldwide. Often they are inherited. When I informed my parents of this, my mom became hysterical, my dad responded with a whipping.

Now here is some irony. Cancer cells don't die; they grow and multiply. Just follow the cells taken from Henrietta Lacks's cervix in 1951.[34]

Programmed or controlled cell death is called *apoptosis*. Lack of *apoptosis* in humans can lead to webbed fingers and toes.

When Caroline told me about her webbed hand, she saved me from myself.

---

[33] "The 'Serpent Seed' heresy revolves around an interpretation of Gen 3:15, which states that there are races of mankind on earth which are directly descended from Satan himself. This doctrine maintains that Satan (the 'serpent') cohabited with Eve and produced a race of tailed men." — Jim Searcy

[34] "Henrietta Lacks's cells multiplied like nothing anyone had seen. They latched to the sides of test tubes, consumed the medium around them, and within days, the thin film of cells grew thicker and thicker. Packaged in small tubes tucked in plastic foam containers, with careful instructions for feeding and handling, shipments of Henrietta's cells went out to labs around the world . . . to Minnesota, New York, Chile, Russia . . . the list goes on. And though Henrietta never travelled farther than from Virginia to Baltimore, her cells sat in nuclear test sites from America to Japan and multiplied in a space shuttle far above the Earth." — Rebecca Skloot, *John Hopkins Magazine*

Cancer, from the Latin meaning *crab*, fourth sign on the astrological band and least visible of the twelve zodiacal constellations, is often identified with evil.

Cancer the Crab was elevated to the heavens for its loyalty to the Goddess Hera after being crushed under the foot of Heracles.

Horary astrology (as opposed to Natal astrology where a person's horoscope is set at his or her birth) establishes the positions of the planets at a selected moment using life-changing events or incidents, or the birth of a question for its calculation point — such as on the morning of July 7, under the astrological sign of Cancer, this: *the rust-coloured specks on my underwear?*

"Louse excrement, or blood resulting from bites," explained the doctor.

Phthirus pubis, or pubic lice known also as "crabs," is an infestation specific to humans that affects the pubic and perianal regions, and sometimes the abdomen, chest, underarms, and head.

He gave me a prescription for Lindane shampoo,[35] along with a list of instructions pertaining to such things as how to treat my eyelashes with petroleum jelly, and how to wash and dry my infected clothes and bedding, so that in addition to the usual post-bathing chores of making sure my hair was evenly parted, and teeth and armpits didn't reek, came the extra responsibility of removing nits with a fine-toothed comb.

---

[35] "Lindane is basically mustard gas, once the crabs ingest it, their lungs collapse and they suffocate to death." — Mark Ames

I shaved my hairy areas just to be safe.[36]

·

---

[36] How else to describe my appearance: In 1976, British glam rocker David Bowie, a.k.a. Ziggy Stardust, played an extraterrestrial in *The Man Who Fell to Earth* — a film about an alien visitor disguised as an Englishman, who comes to America in search of a way to transport water back to his barren planet, only to be left affected by the human condition, sadly betrayed, abandoned, and overcome with alcoholism, a role requiring of him to be skeletally thin and entirely hairless.

Alan Rogers, professor of anthropology at the University of Utah, said: "The record of our past is written in our parasites."

There are two types of crab lice. One type evolved on Homo sapiens. The second type evolved on an earlier human species *Homo erectus*[37] and — given that Homo sapiens will fuck anything — must have transferred during sexual contact.

Dried-up crabs have been found in the genital areas of Egyptian mummies.

Some Middle Eastern tribes harvested crab lice for feasts.

Aztec men flicked them at prospective mates.

Probably, even Jesus[38] had them, considering His special relationship with the penitent Magdalene:[XVI] He who is the patron saint of welcoming hosts.

37

[38] Born "according to the flesh" (Rom. 1:4), and was "in all things like his brethren" (Heb. 2:17).

Not more than a month later, I went back to the doctor; I itched so badly, a reaction to louse saliva. But he wouldn't give me anything because he couldn't find anything.

He warned me that Lindane can be toxic if overused.[39]

Over the summer, I saturated myself with olive oil, mayonnaise, and kerosene, and still I couldn't get rid of them.

I wondered if the crabs that infested Christ had shared His divine nature as I was sharing in Caroline's.

I quit my job, but Estella convinced me to take a leave of absence.

"Do you remember what you told me?" she said. "That if it wasn't for arthritic monkeys we'd all still be swinging from trees. The human race evolved from simian frailties. The definition of disease is to undergo a harmful change. But did you ever consider why our primate ancestors got sick in the first place, that maybe they were just really tired of being monkeys and wanted to be something else?"

---

39 Neurological damage, poisoning, and cancer.

In a dream, I met the man to whom Caroline had given her heart.

He asked if I wanted to feel her heartbeat.

I did. It was strong.

He said: "She saved seven lives — kidneys, pancreas, bone, liver, lungs, and mine."

I said: "People with cancer can't donate their organs. The risk for the donor recipient ending up with cancer is too high."

In the next sequence Caroline appeared, naked, and lying on a table; her flesh was peeled back revealing her internal organs and a perfectly formed frog.[40]

40

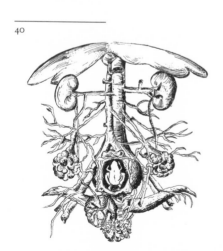

However, a person with a history of cancer can still donate their body for medical science.[XVII]

September 10, 1992: the phone rang in my lap. It was my mother letting me know that Caroline Bayes had been killed in a car crash.[41]

41 "As Newton's First Law of Motion states, an object in motion wants to stay in motion. When you are riding in a car, both you and the car are in motion. When the driver steps on the brakes, the brakes create friction with the car's tires, causing the car to slow down. Usually, if the car slows down gradually, you'll slow down with it. The friction of your legs against the seat, the seatbelt holding you down, your feet pressing against the floor, and other things combine to help you slow down. But if the car stops suddenly, inertia will cause you to keep going forward unless you are somehow tied down, like with a seat belt. So, because of inertia, it's important to wear your seat belt when you ride in a car, to make sure that you stop when the car stops."

"The opposite is true for objects that are at rest. An object at rest wants to stay at rest."
— Tom Snyder Productions

Caroline's funeral was arranged by her father along with the help of her husband.

White flowers only and no mourning. She would have liked that.

At her gravesite, I found a bone, which I later identified as part of the jawbone of a fish. I estimated the length of the fish at over forty metres.[42]

I visited her often and as of November 1, before the year's first heavy snowfall, I'd collected enough bones to build a partial skeleton.[43]

When I watched her funeral again on video I slashed my arms with a water-proof marker. The marker served as a ~~neurological~~ ~~physical~~ ~~mental~~ distraction.

On TV was an old black and white movie, Billy Wilder's *A Foreign Affair;* John Lund was performing the tablecloth trick.

In Grade 6 science class, I'd used the tablecloth trick to demonstrate inertia.[44] Caroline was my assistant. With less than lightning speed I pulled the tablecloth out from underneath a big, glass pitcher of water, and watched in horror as it crashed to the floor.

In Genesis, God promised that water would never again destroy the world.

---

[42] Dating back to the Middle Jurassic period, the Great Plains region of North America was covered by a vast sea. The Great Plains extend from the prairies of Saskatchewan and Manitoba to the grasslands of Kansas. They are the second flattest place on Earth. The abyssal plains are flatter, covering about thirty per cent of the Atlantic Ocean where some believe the lost continent of Atlantis is buried under several layers of sediment.

[43]

---

[44] The actual cause of Caroline's death — "continuity, perpetuity, coiling and uncoiling — the completion of the circle." — Joseph F. Martino, Jr.

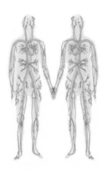

[BOTH SIDES OF LIFE[45]]LOVE[46]

---
45 The word amphibian means both sides of life. This is because the amphibian begins its life in the water and then finishes it mainly on land. An amphibian goes through metamorphosis as it grows from a baby to an adult." — mcwdn.org
46 Original unity.

I grew a beard in the shape of an anchor.

When I sank, I did not want to stop sinking.

In Grade 1, I had a black and yellow bag that resembled a fat wasp. I carried it everywhere.

It was divided into three parts: pouch, zippered pocket, and main compartment.

The body of a yellow-jacket wasp is divided into three parts: head, thorax, and abdomen (in which the stinging apparatus and poison sac are located).

One evening in mid-February, I reached into the bag for my homework. There was a Valentine's card secreted inside, made from construction paper, from a girl named Caroline.

Years later, I dug a hole under the Cancer Tree in Caroline's backyard and buried the bag there, next to Jesus and/or Pinocchio.[47]

---

47 "The resistance of the wood [varied] depending on the place where [Geppetto and the Roman soldiers drove] in the nails: wood is not isotropic. Nor am I; I have my exquisite points." — Roland Barthes

February 14, 1993: in an attempt to overcome my inertia,[48] I bought a map of Winnipeg and circled the spot where Caroline was born.[49] Then I marked an X on fifteen places I held dear.[50]

I connected the dots.

It's the basis of geomancy, a system of divination by drawing marks in sand or on paper and interpreting the shapes. Interpretation is intuitive and doesn't involve complex calculations.

I thought if I concentrated on it hard enough, some meaning would appear but what became apparent was that there was nothing revelatory to be found, like the time I'd stared fixedly at a Laser Art poster and couldn't locate the three-dimensional shape concealed within the two-dimensional picture. (I blamed my colour-blindness.)

Hebrews 11, 1: "FAITH . . . the evidence of things [such as red and green] that appear not. The ~~colour~~ faithblind shall never see God."

---

[48] Immobility, stasis, apathy — the completion of the circle.

[49] O — Misericordia Hospital.

[50] X Her house on Jupiter Bay. X Lord Robert's Community Centre. X Assiniboine Park. X Birds Hill Park. X The Park Theatre. The last movie to play The Park was Brian DePalma's *Phantom of the Paradise,* a flop in every city except Winnipeg. In 1975, during its forty-week run, Caroline and I saw it nine times. X Las Vegas Amusements. X Ralph Maybank School. X Stereo Swap Shop. X BDI or Bridge Drive Inn (Home of the Upside Down Shake). X The Centennial Library. X Fort Garry Library. X Solar News. X The Forks Market, where the waters of the Red River, Assiniboine River and Seine River meet. *Lieu historique national du Canada de La Fourche's* topographical map has a superimposed background comparing Winnipeg's junction of rivers to the rivers of Hades: the Styx, Phlegethon, and Acheron. X Manitoba Planetarium. X Museum of Man and Nature.

On a wintry morning in March, I woke up early (it was still dark) and walked two miles to the bakery to tell Estella that I wouldn't be coming back.

When I arrived, I had such a pain in my side I thought I was going to die.

Estella rushed me to the ~~hospital~~ library where ~~surgeons~~ librarians split me open and removed from under my thirteenth rib a~~n ovarian hematoma~~ large, crumpled wad of paper — pages from books[51] — which they pieced together, and attributed to lonesomeness.

The oldest recorded case in which a man gave birth out of lonesomeness was the birth of Eve from Adam.[52] XVIII

Throughout my library stay, I refused to read and had to be force-read intravenously:

In the days

when you

consumed

what is dead,

you made it

---

[51] A page from every book I'd ever read and ever tried to read.

[52]

what is alive.

When you

come to

dwell in the

light, what

will you do?

On the day

when you

were one you

became two.

But when

you become

two, what

will you

do? 53

They stamped me **Ex-libris** and sent me home *(home is where you* ████ *yourself)*54 along with instructions to avoid sentences with third-person singular pronouns.XIX

---

53 The Gospel of Thomas
54 Her Space Holiday

A tic-tac-toe grid traversed my chest but instead
of X's and O's, I played the game with male and
female gender signs with no winner or loser.
I drew a ~~cross~~ tree on my abdomen.
See how the neck of my uterus resembles my
penis and my ovaries my testicles.
*This is my body. I am the door. Whoever enters
through me will be saved.*

XX

After~~word~~birth

Squaring the Circle

In 1963, before determining the sex of a child born into the range of ambiguous genitalia, (an acceptable sized clitoris is .02 to .09 centimetres, a penis 2.5 to 4.5 centimetres), doctors at the Misericordia Hospital in Winnipeg, Manitoba, were not required — as was common medical practice in the United States — to conduct the following physical exam: a genitourethrogram related to urinary function, a pelvic ultra-sound indicating evidence of the female reproductive tract, a chromosomal breakdown to help establish genetic sex. Instead, doctors at the Misericordia Hospital (re)acted primarily to the parents' wishes, and at those critical moments of decision, the majority of parents wanted boys, though usually the urethras were in the wrong place and scrotums were split, and technically it would have been easier for a surgeon to make the children female than male.

Normal children know their gender identity by age eighteen months.

"The parents must have no doubt about whether their child is male or female — the genitals must be made to match the assigned gender — gender-appropriate hormones must be administered at puberty — and intersexed children must be kept informed about their situation with age-appropriate explanations. If these conditions are met the child will not question her or his assignment and request reassignment at a later age."
— Suzanne J. Kessler, Lesson from the Intersexed

In adulthood, true hermaphrodites are at increased risk of stroke, brain hemorrhage, ovarian cancer, and cancer of the breast. Today, surgery is delayed until the child is old enough to consent.

I — XX

I
The Silver Slippers

The Wizard of Oz's original director Richard Thorpe shot preliminary
footage of Judy Garland wearing silver slippers (in L. Frank Baum's
story the slippers are silver), but neither the shoes nor Technicolor
film stock ever made it into Victor Fleming's finished version. Victor
Fleming wanted Dorothy's shoes to symbolize the vagina, citing the
glass slipper in Cinderella as an example, and so by making the
slippers red they would also come to symbolize menstruation.

"At first the ruby slippers seem like a curse as she tries to escape the
Wicked Witch of the West, but eventually Dorothy comes to
understand their magical power, just as a girl comes to understand the
mysteries of reproduction." — Paul Nathanson, *Over the Rainbow:
The Wizrard of Oz as a Secular Myth in America.*

Today, of the six pairs of shoes made for the film by Western Costume
(MGM's costume department), three are on display in museums
including the Smithsonian Institution, two are in private collections,
and one pair — the silver pair — are rumoured to be on the moon,
left there in 1971 by Apollo XIV astronaut Navy Captain Edgar
Mitchell, grandson of William Jennings Bryan — leader of the
Populist Party and 1896 presidential candidate.

"The Populists wanted bimetallism (the use of both gold and silver) as
the monetary standard. Farmers who joined the Populist movement
embraced the idea of "free silver" as a way of easing the money supply
and giving them better access to credit. *The Wizard of Oz* was written
as a Populist allegory." — Henry Littlefield

The Scarecrow represented the farmer / the Tin man — the industrial worker / and the cowardly Lion — William Jennings Bryan.

"When Dorothy finally gets to Oz (Washington, D.C.) she meets the all powerful wizard (President William McKinley) who is supposed to be able to send her home to Kansas. Instead she finds him to be weak and flawed; in fact he is a charlatan who can only deceive himself and others." — socialstudieshelp.com/Lesson_51_Notes

From 1979 to 1995, agricultural students at the University of Kansas held annual Silver Slipper Parties in the campus' *All Powerful Observatory*, which were free and open to the public. Sadly the size five slippers were just too small and too far away to be seen from an Earth-based telescope. Richard Thorpe was the guest of honour in 1980.

II
Kneel Down on Wood

Acts 5:30 "The God of our fathers raised up Jesus, whom ye slew and hanged on a tree."

Acts 10:39 "And we are witnesses of all things which he did both in the land of the Jews, and in Jerusalem; whom they slew and hanged on a tree."

Acts 13:29 "When they had carried out all that was written about him, they took him down from the tree and laid him in a tomb."

1 Peter 2:24 "Who his own self bare our sins in his own body on the tree, that we, being dead to sins, should live unto righteousness: by whose stripes ye were healed."

Galatians 3:13 "Christ hath redeemed us from the curse of the law, being made a curse for us: for it is written, Cursed [is] every one that hangeth on a tree:"

III
"There's nothing as sad as a man on his back counting stars"
— A Little Argument With Myself, LOW

Out of the twenty-four Apollo astronauts (1967–1972) fifteen of them developed astrocytoma, a type of brain cancer which grows from a group of star-shaped cells called astrocytes. During their space missions they were exposed to intense doses of cosmic radiation; each astronaut received up to an equivalent of 27,000 chest x-rays.

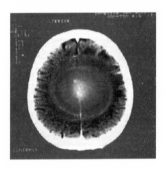

IV
The Secret Language of Mirrors

A construction worker pulled a restroom mirror out of the smoldering rubble of the World Trade Center's north tower. The scorched words on the mirror were in Hebrew SICK DAY TUESDAY.

V
Love Apple

Eve tempted Adam with a metaphorical tomato not apple.

"The tomato plant is hermaphrodite, a perfect plant containing all it needs to self pollinate." — *The Epicurean Table*

VI
"Bomb Affected People"

"The film *The Town That Never Was* [starring Plastic Boy], which for
some reason begins with voices in prayer and the figure of Jesus
covered with blood, describes the uniqueness of Los Alamos
[birthplace of two of the most celebrated mass murderers in world
history, Little Boy and Fat Man] in terms of negatives: no invalids,
no idle rich, no in-laws, no unemployed, no jails,
no sidewalks, no garages, no paved roads.
The film ends with sailors bussing girls on the streets of New York,
and references to the future of nuclear energy and 'rockets to the
stars.'" — Roger Rosenblatt, *Witness: The World Since Hiroshima*

Neither Hiroshima nor Nagasaki is ever mentioned in the film.

Exposure in Utero: the survivors are called *hibakusha,*
"bomb affected people."
Aftereffects: "The head fails to grow while the face continues to
develop at a normal rate, producing a child with a small head, a large
face, a receding forehead, and a loose, often wrinkled scalp. As the
child grows older, the smallness of the scalp becomes more obvious,
although the entire body also is often underweight and dwarfed.
Development of motor functions and speed may be delayed.
Hyper-activity and mental retardation are common occurrences,
although the degree of each varies. Convulsions may also occur.
Motor ability varies, ranging from clumsiness to spastic quadriplegia.
— manbir-online.com/microcephaly

Plastic Boy the Transparent Dummy was used to test levels of
radiation on children after an atomic war.

Notes Toward a Short History of Barbed Wire

provokes anger — *"the Devil's rope"* — used to keep something in (like cattle or Indians) — or something out (like cattle or Indians) — Cherokee Strip — Michael Kelly vs. Joseph F. Glidden — Glidden's Winner (1874) — the Fence Cutting Wars — viscious vs. humane — rips, tears, catches, pierces — smooth rowels which rotate upon contact — Lennox Twist (1883) — Signal Plate (1889) — Jesse James cuts himself on a barbed wire fence — succumbs to infection — was not shot in the back — military applications — foot entanglement — quilting the battlefield — Thin Ribbon Razor Wire used in Vietnam — slices feet, hands, heads, clean off — electrical — torture tool — Roland Penrose's barbed wire bra — Mick Foley loses his ear in a barbed wire wrestling match — National Convention — collectors are called Barbarians — 1500 types — first barbed wire tattoo Hippolyta not Pamela Anderson

VIII
From the Mission Statement of The Flat Earth Society, "Deprogramming the masses since 1547"

Christopher Columbus, using an elaborate set-up involving hundreds of mirrors and a few burlap sacks, was able to create an illusion so convincing that it was actually believed he had sailed around the entire planet and landed in the West Indies, proving the world is shaped not like a pancake, but an orange. As we now know he did not. What Columbus actually did was sail across the Atlantic Ocean to a previously undiscovered continent, North America, and even then only to a small island off the coast. It took him several years more even to discover his blunder and claim it as a "new world." But the damage had already been done, and mankind entered into what we now call its "Dark Ages."

IX

When the Red River overflowed its banks on Wednesday, May 3, 1950, it left behind large amounts of standing water and thirty-eight species of mosquitoes

Winnipeg Community Services posts this warning
during the summer season:
• Avoid ALL outdoor activity near sunrise and sunset.
• ALWAYS wear long-sleeved shirts and long pants.
• Apply insect repellent (containing DEET).
• Make SURE doors and windows are equipped with fine mesh screens.

The following are some diseases that are transmitted
through mosquito bites:

Malaria
Yellow Fever
Dengue Fever
Viral Encephalitis
West Nile virus
HIV? — Winnipeg has the highest rate of
HIV infection per capita in Canada
Hepatitis C? — Winnipeg has the highest rate of
Hepatitis C infection per capita in Canada
Dog Heartworm

X
As close to real magic as it gets:

Psychoactive (magic) mushrooms
and
the basketball abilities of Earvin (Magic) Johnson,
remembering he's still alive and well despite having tested
positive for HIV in 1991.

XI
The Scarecrow to Dorothy in the cornfield:

"They tore my legs off, and threw them over there! Then they took
my chest out, and they threw it over there!"

XII
General Side Effects of Chemotherapy

- Nausea, vomiting, and diarrhea
- Fatigue
- Infections
- Mouth sores
- Taste and smell changes
- Hair loss: often without predictability, sometimes in the middle of breakfast
(hair may grow back a different colour)

XIII
I Spit on Your Grave

The moon is a feminine sphere, when four men landed on her — she
was gang-raped.

cock rocket, cum rocket, man rocket, rocketrod

The automatic vibrator (steam powered) was invented in 1869.
Physicians controlled hysterical women in the late 1800s by forcing
them to orgasm.

1903: Konstantin Tsiolkovsky was the first man to theorize using
rockets as a way to the moon.

heat-seeking missile, love missile, meat missile, morning missile

But Tsiolkovsky failed to notice that male hamsters, during full
moons, spin their wheels faster — past the point of exhaustion.

The female and lunar cycles are linked.

The moon affects the tides, animal and plant life, and the fluids in
men's heads and hearts.

*". . . picking them off one by one and extracting a bloody revenge. The
first is strung up and choked to death, the second gets Bobbited in the
bath, the third gets an axe in the back, and the fourth has a nasty
encounter with an outboard motor . . ."* — review by K. H. Brown

XIV
The same species of moth in which its larvae tunnel
through book pages leaving behind small labyrinths

conceptual fibres
discarded
de-accessioned
often cryptic
smuggled into space
through public dimensions
bookworm
word thief

XV
From Sex Info 101: The Breasts

"Touch her softly, then lift your hand away for a moment, and then
continue. That allows her to have the important moment of
anticipation. Stick to indirect stimulation of the nipples until they
become aroused (hard). Areas that are especially sensitive to touch
include the nipple and areola, the pinkish area that directly surrounds
the nipple [offer words of encouragement if the areola is not
symmetrical]. This whole process should take at least
a few minutes."

XVI
From DiscussAnything.com:

Jeff S.
BANNED

DUDE I WAS LIKE TOTAELLY TALKING TO THIS DUDE I NO ABOUT JESUS
AND I TOLD HIM THET JESUS WAS LIKE A TOTAEL HIPPEAY AND PROBLEY
SMOKED POT ☺ DUDE AND THEN HE SAED THAT JESUS WAS LIKE A
TOTAEL F A G THAT NEVAR HUNG OUT WITH CHICKS AND THET THE
DUDE SPENT ALL HIS TIME WITH 12 OTHAR DUDES IS THAT TRUE DIDENT
HE EVAR HANG WITH CHICKS ☺ DUDE WAS JESUS LIKE REELY A TOTAEL
F A G I HOPE NOT DUDE CUZ HE SURE SEEMED LIKE HE WOODEV BEEN
A TOTAELY COOL BUD TO HAVE ON YOUR SIDE BUT IF HE WAS A TOTAEL
F A G ID SAY NO WAY DUDE

Brainbuster
DA Veteran
Jesus "hung around" with Mary Magdalene, who was a former prostitute.

No, Jesus was not gay.

Jeff S.
BANNED

WOAH GNARLEY!!! DUDE I KINDA THOUT IT WAS A TOTALEY BOGUS
THING TO SAY THET JESUS WAS A F AG BUT I NEVAR WOODEV GUESED
THAT JESUS USE TO SEA A HOOKER ☺ DUDE WAS SHE HOT DO U HAVE
ANY PICS OF HER ☺

Brainbuster
DA Veteran
Cameras didn't exist at that time, but I'm willing to bet she was hot.

Jeff S.
BANNED

DUDE THAT MARY MAGDOLEIAN ☺ SHE HAD TO BE ONE
TOTALLEY TASTEY BABE! ☺

XVII
People for the Ethical Treatment of Cadavers

In 1929 a cadaver received the first neovagina, made with skin from the cadaver's large intestine. In life the cadaver was *Peter Fehlhaber.*

"[There are documented cases of executed criminals] being removed from gas chambers [and electric chairs], and injected with formaldehyde without first being checked for vital signs." — peta.org

Dead African Americans are the most commonly dissected cadaver in the United States followed by dead Hispanics, dead Asians, and dead Caucasians.

Dateline NBC, Jeffrey Dahmer in an interview said: "In 9th Grade, in biology class, we had the usual dissection of frogs, and I took the remains of that frog home and the skeleton of it, and I just started branching out."

XVIII
"Jehovah — genetrix"

"[Until Eve was pried out of him, Adam was a hermaphrodite
creature:] globular, with four hands, four legs, four ears,
just one head, one neck, [Janus-faced]." — Roland Barthes

Plato wrote in his Symposium that mankind descended from a race
of hermaphrodites. The gods split them in two and designated the
divisions female and male.

"Hermaphroditus was the son of Mercury Hermes and Venus
Aphrodite, and had the powers both of a father and mother."
— Ausonius

The word *"sex"* is from Latin *"secare,"* to cut apart.

"The higher meaning of sexual love is nothing other than to help both
man and woman to become integrated inwardly (in soul and in spirit)
in the complete human or original divine image."
— Franz Von Baader

"Herm-friendly"

Genesis 1:27 suggests that Adam did not have a clear and
unequivocal gender identity. The verse states, in the language of its revelation: "va-yivra` `elohim `et ha-adam be-tzalmo, be-tzelem
`elohim bara` `oto, zakhar u-neqevah bara` `otam," "and God created
the man in his image, in the image of God he created him
[`oto, masculine singular, matching the gender of the noun 'Adam'],
male and female he created them [`otam, masculine plural this time,
which can also be used for sets of nouns which include masculine and
feminine nouns]." The shift from "`oto" (singular) to "`otam" (plural)
with reference to "ha-adam" ("the man") is odd and attracted attention.
It is against this background that the following tradition is found:
Rabbi Yirmiyah [Jeremiah] ben `El`azar said: When the Holy One
Blessed be He created the primal man ["the primal Adam"], he created
him an androgyne, and it is therefore said: "male and female he
created them" (Genesis 1:27).

— Intersexuality and Scripture, *FreeEssays*

Some gender-neutral third-person singular pronouns:
heesh
hem
hesh
he-she
himmer
hir
s/he
shim

XX
Archetype

Elsewhere in the Gospel of Thomas, Jesus said: "When you make the two one, and when you make the inside like the outside, and the outside like the inside, and the above like the below, and when you make the female one and the same, so that the male be not male, nor the female female . . . then you will enter (the Kingdom)."

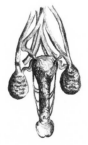

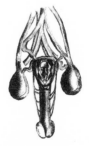

Acknowledgements

Special thanks to: Marcella & Michael Bungay Stainer, Haig Bedrossian & Larissa Lay, Rachel & Amie Merran, Michael Holmes, Crissy Boylan, Rikki Ducornet, Allyson Shaw, Joanne Irving, Peter Fehlhaber, David Butchart, Tim Kieley, Michelle & Mike Cormack, David & Lynda Crilly, and everybody @ This Ain't.

And to: Winnipeg (1963–1996), my conscience is clear.